Tippy The Raindrop©
TM
Thea Klein

Balboa Press books may be ordered through booksellers or by contacting:

Balboa Press
A Division of Hay House
1663 Liberty Drive
Bloomington, IN 47403
www.balboapress.com
844-682-1282

Additional illustration and layout courtesy of Erik MacPeek

ISBN: 978-1-4525-5725-0 (sc)
ISBN: 979-8-7652-5372-4 (hc)
ISBN: 978-1-4525-5724-3 (e)

Library of Congress Control Number: 2012915227

Print information available on the last page.

Balboa Press rev. date: 09/10/2024

BALBOA.PRESS
A DIVISION OF HAY HOUSE

I dedicate this book to my wonderful Mother. Through her I have learned that with great faith, determination and hard work all things are possible! Thank you mother for who you are and everything you have and continue to do for me!

Much Love, Thea

Tippy the Raindrop

This is an interactive adventure story about Tippy the Raindrop, and his dream to rain down to make a flower blossom. Tippy's adventure is interrupted, however, by the Wicked North Wind. Find out how Tippy finds his way and fulfills his dream.

High in the clouds was a raindrop named Tipopulus Raindropulus Ontopovus Aldewet, nicknamed Tippy. That day, Tippy had to decide on whether to drop from the cloud as a raindrop or as a snowflake.

Tippy liked being a raindrop because he could water flowers. He loved flowers and had a special dream of someday making a flower blossom. Tippy knew that if he were a snowflake it would be too cold to make a flower bloom. So he decided to stay as a raindrop and ride on a cloud all day.

As the cloud slowed down, conductor Dusty the raindrop said, "Last stop for all raindrops."

At that, Tippy leaped off the cloud and started his journey to the flowers.

But just then the Wicked North Wind noticed Tippy and said, "Psssst! Hey friend, I know where there are bunches of flowers looking for a raindrop just like you."

"I would like to go, please take me there," Tippy said.

The North Wind whisked Tippy away.

As Tippy rode with the North Wind, he began to get cold and shiver and asked,

"Are we there yet?"

"Not yet, ha, ha, ha," laughed the North Wind.

Brrrrr!

To Tippy's surprise, he saw where the North Wind had taken him...all the way to the North Pole! Tippy had been tricked and was now frozen into a snowflake. Tippy was very sad. Trying not to cry, Tippy got an idea! He would trick the Wind into blowing him back to his cloud.

With a smile on his face, Tippy began to show off as a proud new snowflake. He told the Wind, "I really like being a snowflake, it was very thoughtful of you to bring me here. Now, I am much more beautiful as a snowflake than as a flower."

N
North Pole

Hearing this, the Wicked North Wind became so angry that he blew Tippy all the way back to the raincloud.

"Whew, that was close...I almost lost my dream!"

"Never again will I let anything come between my dream and me," Tippy said.

Weee...

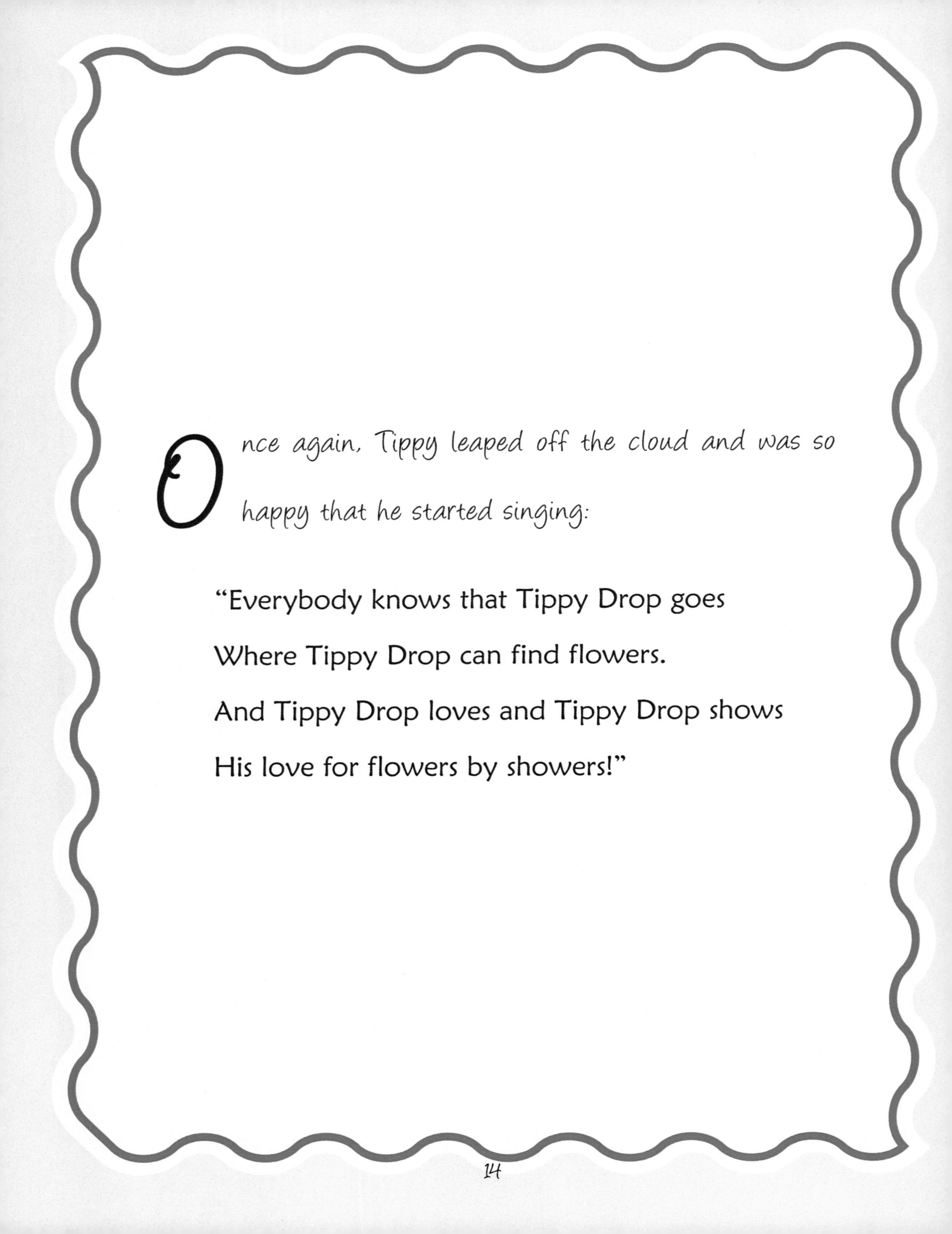

Once again, Tippy leaped off the cloud and was so happy that he started singing:

"Everybody knows that Tippy Drop goes
Where Tippy Drop can find flowers.
And Tippy Drop loves and Tippy Drop shows
His love for flowers by showers!"

At last, Tippy landed on his favorite flower seed and "boing"...up popped a daisy!

Boing!

Tippy Mobile

Color all three pictures (cloud, Tippy the Raindrop and flower), cut them out along the dotted lines, then use either three pipe cleaners or three pieces of string to connect the pictures to make the mobile.

Note: "X" marks the spot on each illustration where the pipe cleaners or string attach. The cloud is first (top), followed by Tippy the Raindrop (middle), and then the flower (bottom). Remember to use one pipe cleaner on top of the cloud so you can hang the mobile.

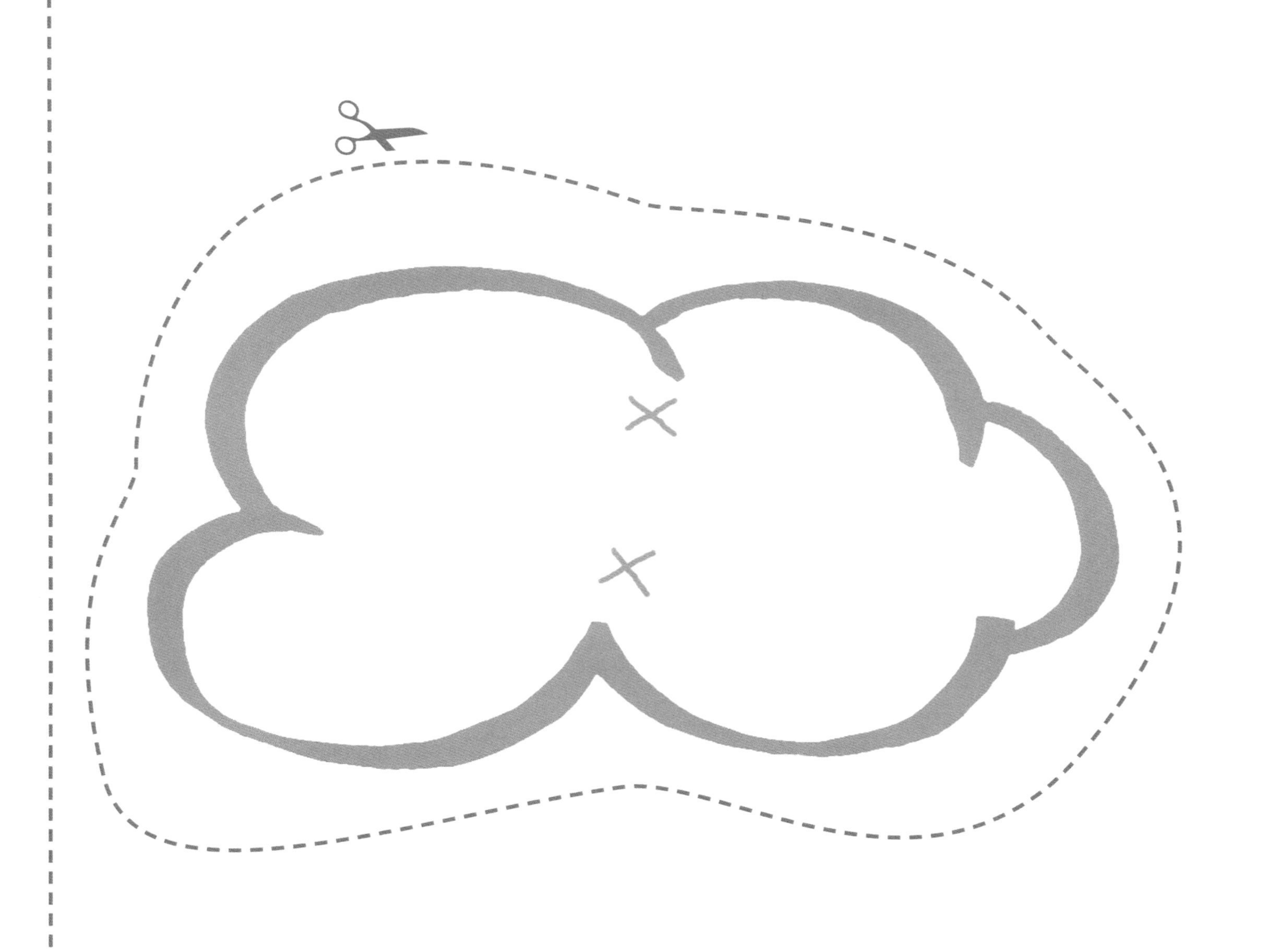

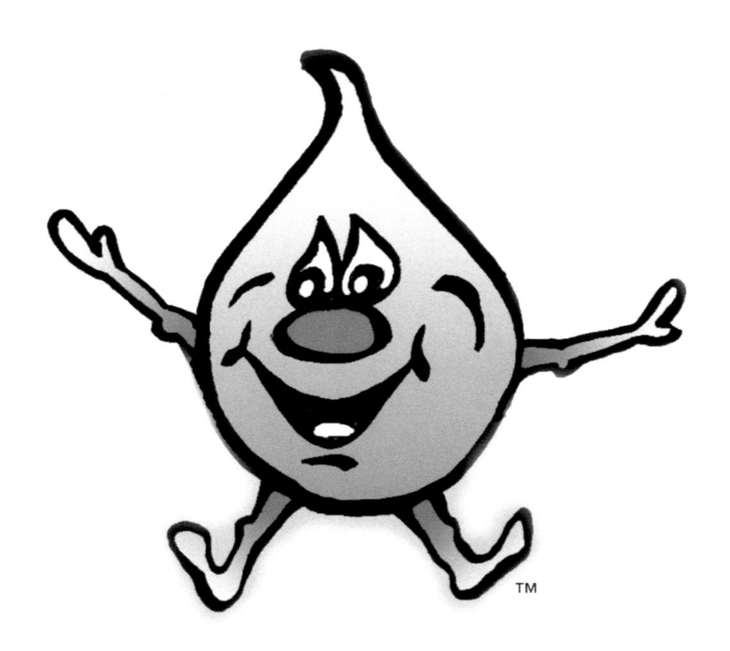